Awakening Wicked

DUCHESS DIARIES BOOK ONE

VIOLET SINCLAIR

HEARTSTONE BOOKS

Cover and formatting by: Skylar Vance

www.skylarvance.com

Contents

Chapter One   1

Chapter Two   19

Chapter Three: 23

Chapter Four: 31

Chapter Five: 41

Chapter Six: 55

Also in the Duchess Diaries Series   77

About Violet Sinclair   79

Chapter One

SURREY, ENGLAND 1816

The best thing about being married to the Duke of Devonshire was he'd died promptly after the birth of their second son.

Lilly dressed in black for the requisite amount of time, but smiled widely on the inside, finally free of the cruel old man. She'd worn lavender for the past six months and refused to wear it one day longer than was absolutely necessary.

She slipped into the silk sapphire gown the color of her eyes. The freshwater pearl necklace shimmered against her peachy skin. Locks of coppery-red curls fell around her face. Freckles stretched playfully across her nose and cheeks. Lips painted red pouted back at her. But she looked weary for a lady of six and twenty.

She'd had many suitors; ten particularly handsome ones. It would've been hard for her to choose... However, the duke wished for her father's lands next to his country estate, and what the duke wanted, the duke paid for handsomely. He bought her father's lands—and her, which netted her father three times what her dowry was worth—not that he'd held on to any of that wealth. The gaming hells were the true winners. Her father passed on shortly after he spent the money, leaving Lillian a hostage at the duke's beck and call.

Thankfully, she had to suffer him once or twice only per month. Five minutes, and he'd leave without a backward glance. He'd often told her that his only prerequisite in a wife was a full set of teeth and wide hips for breeding. Despicable man. She promptly produced an heir and a spare, and the old man keeled over dead.

Even as a debutante, before her father sold her to the Duke of Devonshire like common cattle, no one would have considered her a diamond of the first water, being a mere Baron's daughter. But had her mamma been alive, well, let's just say, the fat old man's whisky breath would never have sickened her nose. Still, now she was thankful. Her life was her own.

She ran her hands down the length of her dress, smoothing the silk over her hips. No more corsets pulling her waist into the size of an orange. After baring a daughter and two sons, it would never fit. Examining herself in the mirror, she'd admitted her hips were indeed wide, wider than on her wedding day.

She cried at the funeral, tears of relief streaming down her face. Anne, Lilly's best and oldest friend, wrapped her arms around Lilly's shoulders, leaned close, and whispered, "There, there. It'll be alright. You're a widow now. We have the most fun," and smiled knowingly. It was true. Widows, especially those left with a fortune the size of the dukes, were afforded certain freedoms, and, provided they were discrete, the ton looked away. Wanton coupling with the most eligible rakes was practically a given. Sex, however, was the last thing on Lilly's mind.

Anne convinced her to attend the three-day house party at Lady and Lord Rycroft's country estate. It was the first she'd attended since putting on black one year ago this evening. It had been a peaceful year with time to read and breathe and stay out of the judging glare of the ton's eyes. Just two nights. She longed to return to her quiet life but had business in London after this affair was complete. She hadn't been in residence at Devonshire House in London since her father died and was not at all looking forward to the horrid trip, necessary as it was.

She wanted only to make her appearances this evening as expected and return to her guest room. Expected. Why had she always done what was expected? Perhaps she will do the unexpected for a change and live a life of a proper lady, alone with her books and needlepoint and tea. Something churned uncomfortably in her belly at the thought. She hated needlework. For the second time this evening, Anne's face appeared in her mind and her voice echoed in her head. "Widows. We have the most fun."

"Oh, my!" Anne covered her mouth with her hand. "You look stunning. I am certain all the rake's eyes in the room will be glued to you."

"Not interested in the slightest," Lilly said tightly.

"Oh nonsense," Anne said. "You can finally do as you please."

"I assure you, dear friend, I am doing exactly as I wish. Enjoying my own company."

A wicked look crossed Anne's face, making Lilly immediately suspicious. "Yes, but you might just enjoy the company of two for a change—or more."

Lilly swatted Anne in feigned horror. And set her eyes on the dance floor. The Marquess of Huntly waltzed by with a young debutante on his arm. Their eyes met and Lilly smiled demurely. What was she thinking? There would be no smiling or flirting and no mindless sex, but apparently the handsome man stirred up something, because suddenly thoughts of him raced through her mind. And she wondered about his brother—or was it two brothers, maybe even three?

This was so not Lilly. What had come over her? Blasted, Anne. Even in her fantasies, she'd imagine steamy sex but not multi-partners. A graphic image of the Marquess plus his brothers swam up in her mind and she nearly staggered with the rawness of it. What had gotten into her?

No one in a long time.

She shook her head sharply, reminding herself to make her appearance and retire early. She'd given up any hope of encounters with passion years ago. And as if the universe itself were against her, their hosts for the next few evenings sauntered across the floor.

No one had looked at Lilly the way Lord Rycroft looked at Phoebe —like a man dying of thirst. Even now, while the whole of the ton watched. Lord Rycroft's blue eyes held a devious twinkle as he danced across the ballroom. Even after all these years, Phoebe glowed and blushed like a new bride every time her husband whispered something in her ear. She wondered what he'd said to turn her cheeks red. Lilly watched as the dance ended and the Lord escorted his wife intentionally away from their guests, settling in the far corner of the room.

Anne bustled over with two glasses of champagne and sat on the sofa. "For you," Anne said, holding the bubbling refreshment toward Lilly. "Come, sit with me."

When had Anne left her side? Had she been so consumed by her own thoughts to notice? Lilly forced a smile and nodded. It wouldn't do to let anyone see her woolgathering, but she didn't take her eyes off Lord Rycroft, who appeared to nibble on his wife's ear.

"Wouldn't you like to get him alone in the gardens?"

Lilly choked on her champagne sucking it in and feeling the burning of bubbles inside her nose. She sputtered and coughed, while Anne patted her back.

"Goodness." Anne inclined her head toward the Rycroft's. "I watch them often, myself. He always looks as if he'd bend her over the settee at any moment."

Lilly sucked in a breath. "You are incorrigible." Then she laughed like a girl still on apron strings.

Anne leaned into the sofa. "Do you ever wonder what our lives could have been like? If we'd chosen differently?"

The question took Lilly aback. As if she'd chosen her deceased husband. As if she'd sentence herself to that existence. Then remembered. She'd never shared—even with her best and oldest friend—the circumstances of her wedding.

Anne, as did the rest of the ton, assumed she'd chosen the Duke of Devonshire for his money and lands and titles. And him being an old man, everyone knew his time would be short in this world and Lilly would be free. Only no one knew what it was like, or that she'd kicked and screamed her way to the altar and cried and thrashed during the brutality of her wedding night. No, no one knew the real Duke of Devonshire, or what she suffered. And as for her, no one ever would. She'd acted and pretended and so would she continue the rouse.

"All the time." Lilly surprised herself with the admission. "I had many suitors, if you recall."

"I do. Ten if I remember correctly—not including the duke. I was insanely jealous, you know." Anne laughed. "Do you remember them all?"

"Yes, most assuredly." She'd committed them to memory, frequently recalling the gentlemen—ensuring she didn't forget even one—entertaining the very dangerous questions of what if... streaming through her mind. She'd been young and stupid then. Worrying over choosing the perfect match—of betraying her heart—and choosing for status as her father wanted.

It was all for naught, and Lilly spent many nights desperately wishing she'd chosen sooner. Perhaps had she not dragged out the courtships... reveling in the attention, her life would have been different. She should have chosen. Any one of them would have been preferable. But she didn't know then how much of a wastrel her father was. Or in how low esteem he regarded his only daughter. A means to an end. That was all she was.

"Let's see," Lilly said, bringing her mind back to the conversation at hand, "there was... the Earl of Abingdon—"

"A terrible rake, but in attendance." Anne craned her neck and inclined her head to show that she'd spotted him. "There, and he's been watching you."

Lilly followed her gaze. Swathed in black save for the white linen shirt and pristine white cravat, Lord Henry Rupert, Earl of Abingdon, was a sight to behold. Raven, unruly locks. A strong face with a sharp jaw, full pouty lips, and deep dark eyes. Broad shoulders and chest tapered to the waist. Powerful thighs perfectly snug beneath his breeches.

Anne sighed. "The man is beautiful."

Lilly sipped on the champagne, attempting to moisten the dryness in her mouth and slow the strumming of her heartbeat. When she was alone, she'd often fantasize about her suitors. What it would've been like had she married one of them? Had they visited her bed chamber. Admittedly, her experience limited her imagination. A problem Lilly was determined to rectify.

Pushing Lord Rupert from her thoughts, she took a deep breath and continued her list. "Mr. Uffington, Lord Melville, Sir Lumley—"

"Married. Married. And married. Who else?"

She chuckled at the seriousness of Anne's face. "Mr. Anthony Boringdon."

"Name matches his personality." Anne motioned with her hand for Lilly to hurry the list along.

"The Earl of Lindsey."

"Eligible."

Lilly swatted Anne. "Lord Derby, Lord Guilford, and the Earl of Crawford."

"Scotland, dreary place. But... I hear Crawford he has certain assets." Anne licked her bottom lip playfully. Her friend refused to give up, insisting she'd join in the ladies of ton's escapades. As intriguing and descriptive as Anne had been with the tales—each more sordid than the last, Lilly could not envision herself in the gardens, or gaming hells, or artist's parties. Or baring her child-scared body for all to see.

"I'm sure you are missing someone."

Anne knew full-well who was missing from the list, and she refused to discuss Philip—Mister Normanby.

"Good evening, Lady Anne." The handsome Mister Crowley, the fourth son of Viscount Crowley, stood before them, his stunning form outlined in the flickering glow of the candlelight. "It's a beautiful evening, is it not?"

Anne practically shot off the sofa. "It is a clear night if I do say so." Her large chocolate eyes shimmered, and her ivory complexion turned positively pink.

Mister Crowley tipped his head. "Ladies." And strolled casually away and through the garden doors into the night. It was the queerest exchange.

"What was that—"

"I must be off." Anne handed the half-full champagne glass to Lilly. "The night awaits. We shall talk after breakfast." Then she winked and practically glided across the room and out into the air.

Lilly swallowed the rest of Anne's glass in one gulp. The bubbles tickling her throat. Then did the same with her own. The drink went straight to her head, spinning her thoughts.

"Another, perhaps?" Came a voice beside her—male, rich, and entirely unnerving.

Lilly turned and met the intense dark gaze of the Earl of Abingdon. He took an empty glass from her hand and replaced it with a full flute. Her gaze traveled up from the top button of his waistcoats to the simply tied cravat, to his graceful throat and his masculine jaw. And was rewarded with a smile of brilliant white teeth. Abingdon raised an amused eyebrow.

A furious blush raced to her cheeks. "I am sure I should not, Lord Rupert."

"Come now," he said, taking the open seat next to her on the sofa and stretching his long legs out before him. Muscular and solid. Lord Rupert slid closer until the heat of his thigh warmed the side of hers most inappropriately.

His scent was intoxicating. Bergamot and brandy—deliciously male. Those eyes smoldered and locked on hers, looking at her in the same hungry manner Lord Rycroft often looked at his wife. And Lilly couldn't believe a man would look at her that same way. Then his gaze traveled over the curve of her nose, rosy lips, and further down to her bosom.

Her nipples tightened, brushing against the thin chemise beneath her gown. A swell of desire filled in her belly. She should have moved away. To a safe distance. She blamed the champagne but sipped from the glass to hide her discomfort. And ignored the moisture pooling between her legs.

"Out of mourning," he said in a low, purring tone. He slid his hand over the sapphire silk on top of her thigh. "The color suits you."

"You forget yourself, my lord," she whispered, sounding as breathless as she felt.

Amusement flicked across his face, followed by desire. Lilly's pulse quickened at the expression in his eyes. It was penetrating and visceral.

Lilly's breathless whisper heated Henry's blood and sent it racing straight to his cock. Christ, woman. He'd been watching her the entire evening, waiting for the opportunity to arise. For Lady Anne to inevitably skirt the ballroom to a liaison in a dark corner of the estate. Henry secretly hoped Lilly would go the way of the rest of the widows of the ton—fucking with abandon, reveling in the nights of pleasure.

Once he'd thought to make her his wife—a lifetime ago—but she'd set him aside for the old Duke and his money. It angered him and the anger only fueled his lust. For a year, he'd waited, not-so-patiently, to possess her. Once he got his hands on her, she'd regret rejecting him with each moan from her delectable lips. He'd show her exactly what she'd missed. Through screams of pleasure. Repeatedly.

Lilly flashed him a coy smile, just slightly upturning of her lips at the corners, causing him to want to run his tongue along the seam. "Meet me in the gardens this night. You won't regret it."

Her plump rose-colored lips pressed together. He imagined those lips wrapped around his cock, her tongue circling his head. Clenching her soft fiery curls, breathing in the scent of her—rose oils and mint mixed with his musk. He'd fucked dozens of women—more—but there was something about Lilly, something he desperately needed. He shifted at the uncomfortable straining against his breeches.

Her eyes traveled downward, fixing on the growing bulge. Her tongue softly moistened her lower lip. A red flush crossed her face and neck and bosom. Pleasant peaks pressing against the silk of her gown. He groaned. Was the minx not wearing a corset?

The way she stared, wide-eyed, lustfully. He was confident a triste in the garden was assured. But when the realization that she was staring at his cock crossed her face, Lilly shot up as if the sofa was on fire, spilling champagne in his lap, highlighting his swollen parts.

Unapologetically, Lilly smoothed out her gown, clearly trying to regain her composure. "Lord Rupert," she said, coolly, "I bid you good night."

The chit stood looking indignant with hands on her hips until he rose, most uncomfortably adjusting his breeches. Fine. Without a word, he stalked toward the smoking room, intending to calm himself. Stung by the rebuff. What did it matter? Plenty of loose women gathered at the Rycroft's. He'd relieve himself of the pressure and forget Lady Lilly.

Chapter Two

Lord Rupert stalked down the long hallway to the men's smoking room, but before he reached the door, Lady Uffington appeared by his side. She smiled widely, her blue eyes twinkling, long golden locks trailing down the sides of her face. Her hand curled around his biceps. "My Lord," she said seductively, "dance with me."

Henry didn't make it a habit to dally with married women, but it was common knowledge that Mister Uffington all but lived with his mistress in the country, and Sandra Uffington did as she pleased. And she did please.

Only this night, Henry couldn't get the sight of Lilly, dressed in sapphire and past mourning, out of his mind. But she'd turned him away, like she did several years ago when she married that old bastard. Still, something attracted him to her, something basal on a primeval level.

"My lady." The earl took Lady Uffington's hand and lead her to the ballroom. At least he would not need to scour the estate for a willing partner, or worse, relieve himself alone in his rooms. Lady Uffington would do nicely.

The charade was always the same. Henry waited an acceptable amount of time before going out the back way to the gardens after the lady left the ballroom. The game of discretion, for show, as every guest in attendance—in the ton—knew how it was played.

The blonde moved into the maze, Henry's feet padding over the grass closely behind until they came to the wall in the rear—a darkened spot he knew well, and where other guests knew not to tread, least they come across an unsuspecting coupling.

Lady Uffington laughed; her head tossed back playfully. "My Lord... you came."

"Oh, I intend to."

In moments, Henry had her back against the wall, his cock straining to be freed from his breeches. Usually, he was a considerate lover, ensuring her pleasure was complete before taking his own. But the sight of Lilly worked him into a frenzy. He'd no patience and longed for release. His cock twitched and his sac tightened and ached.

Uffington's heavy breasts spilled over the top of her bodice as Henry yanked it open. He tilted her head back, lips grazing her throat and making his way down to her breasts. He took a nipple into his mouth. At the sound of her lusty moans, his desperation grew. Her little bud hardened when he circled it with his tongue. He palmed the other, feeling its heaviness, his finger flicking its peak mercilessly. He took her breast deep into his mouth and her hips bucked against him. His fingers found their way between her legs. A gust of heat and moisture met his touch.

She thrust and wiggled, sliding her mons closer to his hand. He dipped inside, stoking her sopping cunt, working her with his fingers, thrusting them repeatedly. Oh, bloody hell. He'd had enough. A moan of protest left her lips when he removed his hands to undo his breeches. But she replaced his with her own. Rubbing circles around her taut little clit.

He freed his cock, and stepped back, fisting himself, and stroking, his blood rushing in his veins. He positioned himself at her entrance and in one strong thrust slid into her wet sheath and his night and frustration over Lilly faded into oblivion.

Chapter Three:

The gall of that man! To suggest she'd throw modesty to the wind and tup in the gardens like a common—like a common—courtesan?

In the last twenty minutes, Lilly swallowed three more glasses of Champagne and clearly, they'd gone to her head because when she'd seen Abingdon slip out onto the open balcony overlooking the gardens, she followed.

His stride was firm, brazen, and purposeful, muscles flexing with each step. Lilly couldn't take her eyes off the snug seat of his breeches, watching how he moved. She'd clearly said no to meeting him in the garden, hadn't she? Or had she said nothing and bid him good night?

A gust of wind blew a stray curl into her face. The coolness of the air whipped beneath the silken gown. Goose flesh raised on her arms, and her breasts tightened at the cold. Lord Rupert took the steps on the right, leading into the darkness below. Not to draw attention, she descended the set on the left and followed at a distance. When he disappeared into the maze, she glanced over her shoulders. No one watched.

Hastening her steps, Lilly pursued the earl. Not thinking of her actions, or what they meant, she slipped between the hedges.

A sharp giggle froze her feet to the ground. She turned back to the party, ready to run from what she'd been about to spy, but the hushed whispers stoked her curiosity. Listening to the breathy moans caused a familiar tightening in her breasts and an embarrassing throbbing between her legs. She glanced around the hedge.

The sight caught her off guard, and she covered her mouth to stifle a shocked gasp. She should've backed away that moment, thankful the couple was too involved to notice her lurking nearby, but her eyes were fixed on their movement.

Lady Uffington's gown was down, exposing her breasts, and Abingdon sucked at them hungrily. Her skirts raised, draping over Abingdon's powerful arms, his hands beneath them, working between her legs. The lady moaned.

A gush of wetness slid down Lilly's thighs. In her whole life, she'd never seen such a sight, or felt so wanton as she did at that moment.

Abingdon unfastened his breeches, and his enormous member sprung free, standing upright, pulsing. Lilly's throat went dry. She feared what she'd see next but was too excited by the display of lewdness to turn away.

Lilly rolled over and tried to block out the images. An impossible task. She'd left the window open to allow the chill autumn air into her rooms. But her skin burned remembering the night's amorous activities. Between her legs throbbed to the non-stop images of Lady Uffington and Lord Rupert.

The shock had been immediate—first hurt with the realization that her company was interchangeable. Then, an overwhelming lustful desire that washed away any feeling of dismay. She wasn't interested in anything resembling a romantic attachment. In fact, she wasn't certain why she followed the retched man. Curiosity. Desire. Need. Envy. Lady Uffington was unabashed, feeling passion and pleasure. And Lilly wanted it all. But the most thrilling—and shocking—was how intensely she enjoyed watching.

She fled the minute he'd slid into the lady. But just then, alone in her rooms, she couldn't help envisioning the outcome. It could have been her, nailed to the wall by the Earl of Abingdon , breathless, and moaning. But she was a coward.

Lilly was in quite a state. She had tossed the bedclothes off for the third time in the past ten minutes. Hot. Tingling. Achy with need. She had half a mind to find Abingdon n's room and demand relief. Attempting to sleep was useless. She walked onto the portico just outside her room.

A light breeze fluttered over her thin nightgown. Looking out over the grounds below, she could hear muted voices, bringing the vision of Abingdon crashing over her once more. Warm brown eyes filled with lust, holding her gaze. His hands strong and sure, pulling her body against his. A shiver ran down her back, sizzling like freezing water trickling over a hot fire.

The married ladies and widows spoke of bedsport as a welcome and pleasurable thing. They enjoyed the liaisons. She dreaded the nights her husband visited her chamber, his hands bruising, his bulk crushed, his retched breath on her neck all while he hurt her unwilling body. When she'd admitted as much to her friend, Anne vividly explained there was something she could do to experience pleasure. Lilly stumbled with anticipation back into her rooms.

A knee clumsily knocked into the night table as she crawled beneath the covers. Her pearl necklace skittering across the floor. She'd tossed them carelessly aside in her frazzled state. Retrieving the cold beads, she set them on the table once again. A gust of wind blew a sweat-soaked curl from her face, and she lifted her hair to cool her neck, but nothing cooled her excruciatingly painful state of arousal. There was only one thing to do if she were to get any sleep. She disrobed, the flimsy nightgown pooling on the floor beside the bed and slipped between the sheets.

From somewhere in her mind, Abingdon's low moans rolled like smooth, round, cool pearls sliding over her taut nub, and suddenly her legs were shaking, inner thighs soaked. The sensation drew her gaze to the night table. Had she really just done what she felt between her legs? Slowly, she pulled on the string, feeling every single icy bead one by one roll over her clitoris. A groan escaped from her throat. Her breast plumped, nipples growing more taut and painful. With her free hand, she cupped her breast and pulled on her pink nipple, imagining Lord Rupert's mouth flicking and nipped until the sensitive skin around it darkened and burned. Her body was growing softer, riper, wanting more--to be full.

She worked the pearls back and forth between her legs, her breath coming in harsh gasps. Heat building, hips rising from the bed, needing something to fill her, to release the pressure. Abandoning the beads, she moved one hand over her own swollen pearl, rubbing and swirling. With the other, she slid a finger inside her wet channel, stroking the silky sides.

Heat flushed up her body. A bead of sweat slid between her heavy breasts. A second finger joined the first, filling and stretching further, pushing farther, hips grinding and bucking to meet the frantic needy rhythm. Her channel pulsing and squeezing. She worked her pearl faster and harder and rocked into her hands. The heat rushed to her head until an erotic scream she didn't recognize pierced the night. Her climax flooding her hands as her body came apart.

Chapter Four:

S lumber kept its hold on Lilly well past sunrise. She stretched, breathing in the cool morning air, the scent of the country wafting through the open window. Sitting up, she noticed a golden square near the door.

She'd fallen asleep quickly, leaving her nightgown abandoned on the floor. Pulling on her thick dressing coat, Lilly padded across the cold floor and picked up the note. Crisp folded paper with the red-waxed seal she'd recognized instantly—Lady Pettiford.

The dowager Countess of Banbury was a force to be reckoned with. The older woman was widowed decades ago and refused to remarry and be shackled to a man. Lilly's stomach tightened. What could she possibly have to say? And why slip a note beneath her bedchamber door as she slept? It was all very unusual, which was one word to describe Lady Pettiford. Others included, tenacious, a fireball, a cat with her claws out. She was like a runaway carriage who would trample anyone in her path—especially if they dared to speak against her or her "ladies." The ladies of the ton who enjoyed her inner circle. As scandalous as Lady Pettiford was famed for being, her loyalty was legendary. But what could she possibly want with Lilly?

Fumbling with the seal, Lilly's hands shook slightly as she unfolded the note.

To the dearest Dowager Duchess of Devonshire,

You are hereby invited to attend the meeting of the ton's most vibrant ladies at Whitterfield's. Instructions will be delivered to Devonshire House during your forthcoming trip to London.

They are to be followed to the letter. Should you have questions, kindly keep them to yourself.

Lady Pettiford

Lilly gasped. The woman was scandalous. Whitterfield's in St. James was a famous gaming hell—a men's gaming hell. What was the woman thinking? And how precisely would the ladies of the ton gain entrance? Dear lord, why would they want to?

Anne waited for Lilly at the entrance of the dining room, smiling and looking positively radiant. "There you are. I've been waiting on you for a quarter hour. I'm absolutely famished." Anne looped her arm between Lilly's and the two ladies crossed the threshold. Lady Rycroft was already eating and chatting animatedly with guests at the far end of the table. Lilly fought to keep her face stoic as she moved past Lady Uffington to the side table.

Sandra Uffington inclined her head, "Duchess." Thankfully, with no sign that she knew Lilly saw her the night before.

Anne scooped a healthy serving of eggs, ham, and pastries onto her plate. "Did you receive your invitation?"

Lilly started dropping grapes from her plate and glanced over her shoulder. "How are they to gain entrance to—"

"No questions." Anne's eyes sparkled.

Lilly followed Anne to the breakfast table setting at the far end nearest to the door. The maid made haste to their side. "Duchess. My Lady. Tea?"

"Oh yes, please."

Most of the men had left for a hunt early that morning, led by Lord Rycroft. A relief. Perhaps she'd be able to steer clear of Abingdon for the next two days. The room filled with ladies save for Viscount Walsby, whose gout was acting up, and Mr. Crowley, to whom Anne made multiple sideways glances. "Lillian is heading to London when the party breaks," Anne said to Mister Crowley. "Perhaps I'll join her."

"You must stay at Devonshire House." Lilly sipped a spot of tea. "It'll be wonderful to have a friend. You know how I despise going to London during the season. It's a dreadful bore."

"I would love to stay."

"It's settled then. You will travel with me to London tomorrow afternoon."

Anne clapped her hands. "Splendid. We shall have the most fun." Perhaps for the first time in six years, London will hold some excitement. At the very least, she and Anne would enjoy each other's company. They were still close but could not spend time together as they once did. They had been practically inseparable—until her husband regulated her to their country estate with only the servants and her embroidery. Out of boredom, she'd employed Mister Fitz, who instructed her in archery each week.

"What is settled?" The familiar masculine voice came from the doorway. Abingdon strolled into the breakfast room, heading directly for the side table. "What have I missed?"

"I beg your pardon?" Lilly felt her face flush. Dear lord, why did this man have the effect he did upon her? Blushing like a girl in the schoolroom. 'It's impolite to intrude upon one's conversation."

Abingdon chuckled. "My apologizes, Duchess. I'm merely curious as to Lady Anne's excitement."

"I shall go to London with Lilly tomorrow noon," Anne said. "And we shall have a smashing good time."

"London." Abingdon raised an eyebrow. "You ladies in London without escorts?"

"Excuse me Lord Rupert." Lilly sat up straight. "We do not require—"

"My lady. I make a gest." Abingdon took the seat directly across from Lilly and smiled as if he knew how uncomfortable he made her. "You are leaving early, then." He popped a slice of ham into his mouth, chewed, and never took his eyes off her.

"Only by a day," Lilly said. "I've matters to discuss with my husband's solicitor."

"Your late husband," he corrected, his full lips sipping the tea.

Good God, woman, why are you staring at his lips? Because she remembered how they nibbled and sucked and teased. Shaking her head to clear the thoughts, she elbowed Anne's teacup. It tipped from the saucer, tea spilling across the pristine tablecloth.

"Oh dear." Lilly dabbed the liquid with her napkin.

The maid rushed from her position next to the side table. "Don't trouble yourself, your grace."

"I've got it," Lilly stammered. "Truly." But then, in her haste, her hand came down on Anne's fork, sending it flying across the table. It clattered and tumbled for what felt like an eternity, flicking fluffy bits of eggs across Abingdon's cravat. "Oh... oh... no..." Air, she needed air. There must be out-of-door activities set up for the ladies to take part. She needed to leave.

"My apologizes, Lord Rupert." She grabbed Anne's elbow. "Didn't you say there was archery? Shall we go? Immediately?"

Lilly didn't wait for an answer. She moved toward the door, begging her feet to slow down so she wouldn't look as if she was running from the room, running from him.

Too much brandy and too little pussy caused Henry's midmorning waking. He'd been in a foul mood, realizing that while he slept the men left for the hunt. He wasn't at all surprised. Lord Rycroft waits for no man.

And learning the ladies were leaving the house party early for London, did nothing to help his disposition. His pulse sped. How could he just let her go running off to London? Clearly, they had had a connection. A sensual longing. He saw it in her eyes. There was no doubt in his mind she wanted him.. He moved quickly to sit, to hide his arousal beneath the table. Just being in the same room with Lilly did all kinds of things to his body. But she was leaving—tomorrow—his time was running out. If he was to possess her, to sample what he'd missed, to hear the Duchess of Devonshire screaming his name, begging him to bring her to climax, today was his only chance.

She'd said she had a meeting with her husband's solicitor. Why'd he felt the overwhelming need to correct her, to remind her the duke was dead? He didn't know. Nor did he know why the bloody woman continually ran away.

Chapter Five:

The wind whipped through Lilly's hair as she pulled back the string of the bow. She took a deep breath, and with the exhale, loosened the arrow. It flew true, hitting the target dead center with a clunk. She needed to gain hold of herself. Making herself a complete fool over breakfast. The blasted man unnerved her. But the bow, that was calming. When she was a child, her father had taught her, and she'd had plenty of time to practice when her husband was in London. He'd taken her less and less over the years, for which she was eternally thankful for the reprieve.

"Jolly good shot!" Mister Crowley said, cheering Lady Anne's horrid effort. "Do try again."

Anne squealed in delight. "I fear I need pointers. Don't you agree, Lilly?"

Lilly laughed. Growing up with Anne and spending many summers in their country estates, she knew Anne was a more than adequate marksman, and quite a shameless flirt. Mister Crowley must have enjoyed Anne's company the night before to forego the hunt.

"Yes, Mister Crowley, Anne is just horrid. Lend her your talents."

Crowley arched an eyebrow. "You, Duchess, are a splendid shot. Right center."

"You're very kind." Lilly drew another breath, pulling the string and rested her palm against her cheek.

"I would gladly lend you my talents, Duchess." Abingdon's voice was close—too close—so close his hot breath caressed her jaw.

Lilly started and released the arrow along with a whoosh of air from her mouth. It clunked into the grass, head down several yards away. Insufferable man.

"I do not require your assistance, my lord." She grabbed another arrow.

"I beg to disagree."

"I was doing fine before you arrived." Lilly hastily drew the string.

Abingdon put a steadying hand on her arm. "Keep your elbow raised." His hand ran the length of her arm, resting over on hers. "Take a deep breath," he murmured, his mouth grazing her neck just behind her ear.

She froze, not wanting to cause a scene. Or pull away from the closeness and the heat of him. Closing her eyes, she let out the breath and loosed the arrow.

"Exquisite. Just like you in this dress," he said.

The flutter of pleasure that his words registered down low in her stomach horrified Lilly. The heat crept lower. If he was worried about a scandal, he didn't show it.

"Duchess, I am gripped by desire." He pressed closer. "What say you? Have you changed your mind? Will you meet me this eve, before you return to London?"

Wetness flooded her draws remembering how she'd fantasied about him the night before, how she ran her fingers along her taut pearl. She'd felt nothing like it before—and the sudden realization that she yearned to feel the sensations again—and much more-- turned her legs to gelatin.

"I did it!" Anne jumped up, clapping her hands, and it broke the spell.

Lilly pushed away from Lord Rupert. "I think not, my lord." She tossed down the bow and stalked toward the lake.

The man was impossible. Meet him? No, she would not. She had followed him, despite herself. Likely would have given herself over to the desire, but he was with Lady Uffington—and a married woman. Yes, she was a widow, and the ton would look the other way. In fact, Anne would be positively pleased, and Lilly had been curious if what her friend and the other married woman said was indeed true. Could sex be something to look forward to? Pleasurable with a man? Honestly, she couldn't imagine it being so. But Abingdon's nearness did things to her body that she didn't think possible. And she was curious. But did she have the courage to act on it?

Henry could have any widowed lady in attendance, of that, he was confident, but from the moment he'd seen Lilly the night before, fresh out of mourning in the stunning sapphire gown, he'd wanted her. To run his lips along her alabaster skin, his hands through her silk coppery curls, his lips teasing her heart-shaped mouth. Last night he'd occupied himself promptly to forget about her, but that morning when he spotted her in the breakfast room all the desire came rushing back and shot directly to his cock, apparently.

She'd run out on him at breakfast, and now stormed off angrily, discarding her bow. And tomorrow, his chance would pass, and Lilly would be gone off to London, joining Lady Anne and the rest of the widowed ladies of the ton to take part in their debauchery—or at least he'd like to imagine her participation.

Lilly moved quickly, skirting the lake. He could see her holding the bottom of her dress bearing her ankles to allow herself to move faster. She made her way further from the estate house, further from him. Henry practically sprinted to reach her.

"Duchess. Duchess. Lilly, wait."

She glanced over her shoulder, her perfectly plump lips pressed together as if she considered stopping before turning and continuing her path along the waterside. Bloody hell.

He quickened his feet, almost excited by the pursuit, and caught her by the elbow. "Blasted woman, why do you keep running off?"

"Unhand me."

The vehemence in her voice took him aback, but he was undeterred. He pulled her closer, her breasts pressing against his chest. "I know you want me. There's no denying. I see desire in your eyes, Duchess."

"You, sir, have an overactive imagination. You see no such thing."

"Don't I?"

She tried to pull away, but he held her tight. "If you don't want me, then why so angry?"

"I saw you," she said, lifting her chin. "In the gardens last night."

Henry released her. "So, you came? To meet me?" Blood rushed straight to his cock. It grew thicker and harder, pressing against his breeches. His jaw clenched.

"No... " she stammered, "I—I merely needed some air and there you were all... entangled. And with a married woman!" She'd denied her reason for going to the garden, but the truth was plain on her face.

He loomed over her, swiftly grabbing her shoulders and moving back to duck behind a tree. Her feet stumbled, but she didn't pull away. The scent of grass and impending rain enveloped them as he pressed her against the hard bark. "Mrs. Uffington, as you well know, does as she pleases. And you, Duchess cast me aside if you recall."

Lilly's eyes blazed. "I did no such thing. I simply declined a mindless roll in the gardens with a notorious rake."

"A rake?"

"Through and through."

Henry pressed his lips near to Lilly's ear. "But you didn't decline, did you, duchess? You very much desired a roll with a rake as you say. Otherwise, you'd not followed me into the gardens."

"Regardless—"

He captured her mouth, his tongue teasing the corners until she was kissing him with a passion and abandon that riveled his own. He pulled away, looking down at her swollen lips. "I was only with another to erase you from my mind, Lilly. Ever since I saw you yester evening I can't stop thinking of you."

His hands spanned her waist, and he sank into her, bending his knees so his hips aligned with hers as he pressed his manhood against her. "See what you do to me, Duchess?"

Lilly gasped, her eyes wide and disoriented.

His lips slid along the line of her jaw. She smelled intoxicating, like rose oil and lavenders and something distinctly sensual. She tilted her head back, her hands gripping his biceps tightly. Her breath caressed his ear.

He claimed her mouth in a crushing kiss, his hips grinding against hers as his tongue swept her lower lip, demanding entry. She opened for him, as he imagined her legs opening. He wanted to fuck her right against the tree in full view of anyone who could happen upon them.

Lilly's hands came up to his shoulders, and she clung to him, returning his kiss with a fervor matching his own. But the kiss told of an innocence—a lack of experience—he could not explain. She threw herself at him with wild abandon, and he wanted her. His every muscle taut and coiled.

Pressing her further against the tree, he slid his hand up her waist and over her ribs, cupping her breasts through her gown. "God, woman, are you wearing nothing beneath your frock?"

She moaned against his mouth, her breath coming in swift gasps. He jerked the gown down, exposing her nipples, pink as roses, and rolled the peaks between his thumb and forefingers. His mouth trailed a path down her neck and then further to her breast, his tongue making circles around one nipple, while he massaged and flicked the nipple on her other breast. She cried out.

"I want to undress you and lick every inch of your body. Then I'm going to fuck you. Would you like that?"

She arched her back and pressed her body more fully to his. He grinned, reaching down to cup her arse. He pulled up her skirts and nudged her legs apart with his knee. Her hips moved forward to meet him. He ran his hand up her leg, tracing tiny circles on the soft skin of her inner thighs. The sounds he drew from her encouraged him to move further, slowly. He'd prolong the torture. His palm found her mound, massaging it with small circles. "First, I'm going to make you come." His voice was so rough with desire, he'd wondered if she'd understood his words. Her tongue darted from her mouth, moistening her lower lip, and he was almost undone. "Do you want that, Lilly?"

He ran a finger along her folds, over her draws, and worked them aside. Her legs weakened, but he held her firm. "You like it? Ask for it."

"Yes. I want it," she said, breathless. "Please."

He played at the curls, moist and warm, and parted them to find her swollen nub. She moaned as his index finger slid over it, lower and lower, gliding over the folds and back again, circling her hidden gem. His cock strained painfully against the fabric of his breeches at the feel of her heat, slick and wet, desperate for release. But he'd wait, make her want it—beg him for it. He dipped a finger into her tight sheath, then joined it with a second. "You're so wet."

Lilly moaned, the sound spilling out of her wild and wanton. Her hips thrust forward, fucking his fingers. He consumed her lips, fingers thrusting in and out of her. His thumb slid through her curls again, finding the swollen bit of flesh that would make her scream and stroked it mercilessly. Her thighs clenched together, as to not let him go, and she moved in sync with his pumping fingers. "That's it, come for me."

She gripped his shoulders, the walls of her channel spasming, gripping his fingers tight, and he'd imagined how that sweet cunt would feel gripping his cock. He felt the pulsing in his groin. Soon enough.

When Lilly stopped shuttering, Henry removed his fingers from her and raised them to her lips. "Open for me, love," he purred. "I want you to taste your pleasure."

Her eyes still lidded with passion, she parted those luscious lips, and he inserted his fingers dripping in her juices into her mouth. She licked them and sucked them. So erotic was her mouth on him, he feared he'd spend himself within the breeches.

He removed his fingers from her hot mouth and slowly reached beneath her skirts. He found her swollen clit and rubbed. Lilly jerked away, but he held her tight, swirling and rubbing until her breathing was hard and she cried out for more.

"Do you want me, Lilly?"

She nodded and pumped her hips. Any pretense or protestation gone, overthrown by her passion. He'd possessed her thoroughly.

"Say it. Say you want me to fuck you." He worked between her legs harder and, with his other hand, pinched her darkened rosy nipple harder than before.

"Oh!" She bucked against him. He pinched again. "Oh, my—"

He slipped two fingers into her sopping cunt, joined it with a third. He played the insides of the sheath, finding the spot he knew would cause her to come apart in his hands again. "Say it, love."

Lilly's voice was terse and her breath heavy. "Yes. Yes, please."

He reached that lovely spot, and she screamed. "Please, what?"

"Please." Her voice was barely discernable. "Fuck me."

He teased her to the brink of orgasm, then removed his hand at once, and she cried out and quivered desperately for release. Pressing his pulsing erection between her legs, he dragged his lips across her neck and lightly bit the lobes of her ear.

"Abingdon ..."

"Shh," Henry purred, thrusting his hips. "You want this?"

"Yes." She clutched at his arms, pulling him closer

"Midnight. You will meet me here at midnight."

He released her and his cock protested at losing her heat, but he'd take care of it in his room. He couldn't very well fuck the duchess out in the open next to the lake in broad daylight—or perhaps he could have, but he'd wanted her to anticipate their night. To need it, to think about his cock at dinner, for her panties to be wet for him while she sipped her wine and made polite conversation.

Then, he'd fuck her in a frenzied rush, hard like she'd begged until she screamed his name into the night. Then he'd lick her sopping cunt and turn her over... Henry picked up the pace before he didn't make it to his chambers.

Chapter Six:

Lilly absolutely, positively, was not meeting the retched man at midnight. Besides, she'd be horrid at discretion. Dinner was an uncomfortable moist affair, with an embarrassing throbbing between her legs, causing her thighs to squeeze together. She pushed the earl and his illicit proposal from her mind, but the more she pushed, the more she imagined him pushing the length of him into her. Good God. Her mind was lost.

Lady Anne could let nothing go and had asked what matter of meeting she enjoyed with Abingdon after her abrupt departure from the archery lawn.

Heat rushed across her face. "Nothing happened."

Anne's eyebrow arched, and she nodded. How on earth would she hide her activities from the ton, if she could not answer one simple question—two words—with untruth?

After dinner, and dancing, and dallying, Lilly asked Lady Rycroft if a bath would be possible. The footman delivered the copper tub to her chamber, followed by several servants carrying steaming buckets of water. Soaking in the steamy water was just what she needed to soothe the stress of the day, and her insistent need. Abingdon was an insufferable creature, bringing her to the brink, insisting she asked him to... she sunk deeper in the tub. Ready to die of the embarrassment.

At quarter past eleven, Lilly stepped out of the chilling water and dried in front of the roaring fire in the hearth. Thoughts of Abingdon swirled about her head like champagne bubbles in the too many glasses she'd consumed that evening.

In the mirror, she examined her naked form, the swell of her stomach, and tattooed marks of child birthing scars. She traced her finger across her bellybutton. Self-conscious of the way she looked disrobed. But the night was dark, and pleasure awaited. Who was she fooling? Even as her mind protested, her treacherous legs would take her to the lake. There was no use fighting it.

Outside her window, the guest's laughter and chatter reached her chambers. Most were still reveled in the party below. She'd need to avoid them.

She reached for her chemise and frock, but a thought of absolute insanity gripped her, and she tossed the frock aside. Then she pulled an emerald velvet cloak around her shoulders and slipped out the chamber doors. Lilly covered her still damp hair with the thick hood and made her way down the servants' stairs, praying no one would recognize her.

Once free of the estate, she quickly slipped into the gardens, weaved in and out of the maze of hedges, and past the wall to the fields and lake beyond. The night was pitch black save for the glowing moon peeking through the mounting clouds.

Certain that footfalls followed, she increased her pace. Reaching the rendezvous point, the reality of the situation hit her. What if it was not Abingdon's footfalls but another of the ton's following her—or worse an untoward gentleman looking to do untoward things?

Her breath hitched in her throat, and she moved swiftly.

Beneath the tree lay a blanket spread languorously across the lawn, a bottle of wine and two goblets. She turned in a circle—no Abingdon . Gooseflesh broke along her arms in the cold air. She listened intently. The footfalls seemed to have stopped. Where was the bloody man? She pulled the cloak tighter against the chilly wind and considered returning to her room.

Instead, Lilly moved toward the blanket and sat in the center, stretching her legs out in front of her. She'd wait a few minutes and poured herself a drink to calm her nerves.

From behind a nearby tree, Henry watched Lilly break free of the gardens and enter the clearing, Crowley trailing several feet behind. He'd worried the gent would happen upon her, but thankfully, he'd made a swift left and darted into the darkness. Henry was uncertain just how adventurous the dowager duchess would be. His muscles tightened. He'd reveled in the thought of another watching him fuck Lilly until she begged for release. Blasted! His cock was rock hard.

He approached the place she sat waiting and stopped a few paces from her. She had opened the bottle of wine and was gulping it hungrily. "Lilly."

Her tongue darted out to wet her lips, and she lowered the hood of the cloak. Her soft red hair spilled over her shoulders. "Abingdon "

"Henry. I'd say we are beyond formality, are we not?"

"Henry," she said, her breath fractured. Desire clear in her eyes.

Everything about her was delicious, full lips, ample breasts, rosy, pink nipples and lush, lush hips. It took all his strength not to take her at that moment. To push her on her back and fuck her into the ground. He reveled in the thought of sinking into her body and enjoying her until he was spent.

He crawled across the blanket and buried both his hands in her hair, consuming her mouth with his. The sweet hint of wine intoxicated him. Grabbing his shoulder, she pulled him closer, deepening their kiss. He groaned, almost inaudibly.

He covered her with his body, pressing the length of him against her belly. She was warm and willing. She pulled at the string of her cloak, pushing it aside to find only a thin chemise beneath. "You minx. Where is your frock?"

Her chest rose and fell with each breath. "I had no need of it."

He moved his hand to cup one of her full round breasts through the thin material, flicking a taut nipple through the chemise . She tossed her head back and wriggled beneath him. The friction overwhelmed him, and he needed to put distance between them before he could no longer contain his desire. He had plans for Lilly, and he was not so green as being unable to contain himself.

He reluctantly pulled away. Lifting himself, he sat back on his knees. "Not yet. I want your skin bare, and the air to blow across those gorgeous nipples. Remove your cloak."

Slowly, Lilly sat upright, and glanced from side to side. Bloody hell was the minx self-conscious now after leaving her bedchamber in a chemise? He reached slowly over her for the wine bottle and goblets. Poured two glasses and setting hers aside, he took a gulp of the sweet drink.

She shrugged the cloak from her shoulders and shivered.

"Good," He purred. "Now the rest. I need to see the wares I'm sampling."

She hesitated, but then reached for the bottom of her chemise and yanked it up.

"Slowly."

Lilly stilled, and then slowly slid the gown over her creamy thighs. Further still revealing her sweet cunny. Good God. He sucked in a breath. The woman left her rooms with no small clothes. The thin material slid over her soft middle and finally freed her ample breasts.

"Toss it," he said, inclining his head toward the lake.

Her eyes widened, but she obeyed. "Now, lay back and spread your legs." She did.

"Good gel." He looked at her perfect cunt, glistening with moisture in the moonlight. "Beautiful."

The autumn night air was freezing, but Lilly's body burned. Heat flushed her cheeks and chest. Abingdon —Henry was sure and commanding, looming over her with his muscular legs, and then he kissed her, and his hands were everywhere at once. And when he commanded her to undress, she'd obeyed without a word. In fact, she found she rather enjoyed his taking charge.

Henry wedged himself between her splayed legs, fully clothed. But she felt the evidence of his desire, hard and thick. He ran his fingers along the skin of her upper thigh, teasing the crease there and sending tingling delight straight through to her core.

Her hips pulsed under his touch. She sighed, and she felt him stroke lightly over the curls of her mound. Henry made a groaning sound deep in his throat, his eyes fixed on her. "I want to kiss you..." He ran the knuckles of his hand down her seam, pressing down slightly. "Here."

She bolted upright. "What? You cannot."

Understanding dawning in his eyes. "Am I to understand? No one has ever..."

She shook her head, a wave of panic mixed with the intense desire. His lips on her, there. No one had kissed her cunny. Her late husband, thankfully, didn't kiss her at all. Never had she imagined it could be like this... feel like this.

Henry groaned. His fingers slid between her folds, touching that place she ached for him. "Lay back," he commanded.

The ball of anxiety subsided, and she nodded and sucked in a harsh breath, her chest heaving as he explored with his fingers, swirling in circles around her entrance and sliding up to rub the pearl nettled at the top. "Do you like this, Lilly?"

"Yes, oh yes." Her hands bunched the blanket, gripping at it to keep herself from floating to the stars. She pulled him closer as he worked his magic, desire flaring to desperation.

"Good," he whispered, pressing down harder, making her cry out with pleasures and sending a rush of slippery wetness over his fingers. He lowered himself between her legs, nudging her thighs gently, opening her further. She shivered as he blazed a trail of furious kisses over her soft stomach. Then, to her amazement, he moved lower, tickling her folds and running his tongue up and down.

She arched her back and pressed her need into his mouth. Her inner thighs tensed as the pressure built and built, heat coursing through her veins, setting her on fire. She moved with his tongue, up and down. He flicked it from side to side on her taut pearl, sucking it into his mouth. The intensity threatening to send her over the edge.

Releasing her grip on the blanket, Lilly clutched at Henry's hair.

"That's right. Guide me where you want it." His voice vibrating against her sensitive spots, sending intense shocks of pleasure into her belly and down her legs.

He slid a finger between her folds and into her channel, then followed it with another. Her walls gripping and pulsing as he pumped them harder. Her hips rocking. His tongue swirled and licked. Lilly pressed herself into him hard, desperately lifting and lowering her hips, sliding her slick cunny across his tongue, faster and more desperate.

"Oh, god," she cried, the throbbing pressure unbearable as her body rose and fell. Pressure and heat rising until she tumbled over the edge and shattered. Ripples of bliss and release washed over her like she'd never experienced. More than her own touch had ever accomplished.

Henry trapped her screams with his mouth, consuming her lips and girding his arousal between her legs. The friction drew a violent shutter, nearly launching her off the blanket had his body not held her to the ground. Then he released her, and she moaned at losing him.

Lilly watched mesmerized as he released his thick manhood from his breeches. It sprung free, standing upright. She moistened her lips with her tongue and swallowed her instant nervousness. My lord, it was tremendous.

Henry fisted the base and stroked up and down.

An involuntary moan broke free of her throat, and her cunny pulsed desperately.

He dragged the engorged head against her slick folds, sliding it up and down across her swollen flesh. He rubbed his length over her taut, sensitive pearl.

He placed his manhood at her opening, positioning himself. She tossed her head back, rocking against him selflessly. She needed him to fill her, to push deep and fulfill the desire building. The retched man gritted his teeth and moved away.

"Ab—Henry, please."

"Show me where you want it, Duchess," he said, stroking his impressive member slowly up and down, stirring up more lust than she'd ever felt.

She moved a single hand between her legs. "Here." The pressure was becoming more unbearable, if he didn't take her now, she would scream.

"Ah, and are you ready for me, my dear?"

Before she could answer, voices sounded nearby--male and female. "Oh, my god—" Her breath caught, and she frantically tried to cover herself with the cloak should the couple happen upon them, but Henry moved too swiftly, snatching the cloak and tossing it aside.

"Oh no, don't cover that sweet cunny," he purred.

"But someone may—"

"Let them watch." Their eyes locked and Henry smiled. "Or listen to your ravenous screams of pleasure."

The familiar ball of panic swirled around her belly, threatening to take hold and cause her to flee to her bedchamber behind the safety of the doors. But another sensation overthrew the anxiety-filled fear—excitement. She knew it was wanton but couldn't find the will to care.

Then a series of not-so distant passionate moans began, and Lilly was undone. Her inhibitions replaced with something else, wild and free. She leaned back on her elbows. "As you wish, my lord."

God, yes. Under the moon, hot, wet and wild. The look in Lilly's eyes as she reclined, pushing her gorgeous breast toward him as a feast, nearly caused him to cum right there all over them. He moved swiftly, covering her with his body. The other couple's moan grew louder, mounting to the crescendo he knew well. They couldn't have been more than a couple yards away and the thought set his cock pulsing.

He teased Lilly's opening, and she grabbed his shoulders, but he took her wrists and held them down over her head. All at once, he moved, flipping her to her belly, splaying her legs with his knees and spreading her arms out over her head. His hard length pressed against her arse.

"What are you doing?" she hissed.

Releasing one arm, he slid his arm beneath her stomach and lifted her until she was on her hands and knees with that gorgeous glistening cunt open for him. "Giving you what you begged for, duchess."

"Like this?" The question he knew was meant to sound indignant, but it was breathy and excited and filled with lust that rivaled his own. It made his cock harder than ever before. He wanted to sink into her soaking body.

"Oh yes, like this, and so many other ways." His palm found her mound, and he kneaded it. With his other hand, he reached around grasping a lush breast and tugged at the hard pebble. She let out an almost inhuman moan into his hand. "You like it outside where everyone could see—or hear."

She pressed her arse back against his member, a chorus of wanton sounds leaving her throat. "Yes, that's it, my wicked widow."

Lilly had never dreamed of being so wicked, and at that moment she couldn't think of one reason why not.

Oh god, yes! Crowley. Harder.

Lilly's pulse tripled at the erotic screams. She pressed her hips back toward Henry, wanting him to take her... to take her like she could hear Crowley taking Anne. She should not intrude on her friend's liaison, but her body had other plans. The pure erotic sounds and cries of pleasure excited her, sending a fevered rushing of blood through her veins.

And when Henry whispered, "spread your legs apart and lift your arse so I can push into that beautiful cunny of yours," she complied without a care in the world, giving herself over to her naughty pleasure. The world be damned.

She looked over her shoulder at the earl, his shape dark and brooding against the moonlight. "Please."

Henry placed a hand on her back, gently nudging her down to her elbows. Crawling over her, with his erection in hand, positioned himself at her opening and with the other guided her back onto his shaft. She wriggled and pushed back, trying to take him fully inside. She stretched her arms forward, her breast resting on the blanket like a feline in heat. It was more than he could bear.

In one quick thrust, he buried himself to the hilt in her tight, wet pussy. She called out in pleasure, and his excitement built, thinking she'd draw the attention of Crowley and Lady Anne. He hadn't heard them in a few moments. Lilly ground her hips back against him, begging for movement.

He pulled his glistening cock back, sliding it almost out past the folds before thrusting forward. With hands on her hips, he continued in and out until he filled her to capacity and his sacs slapped recklessly against her arse. But he wasn't ready to spend himself just yet. He thrust forward, gritted his teeth, and stilled. Her walls pulsed and gripped his cock. Lilly rocked forward and back, trying to continue the rhythm, but he held her tight in place and reached around her waist, thumbing her pearly button. She moaned and called out, trying to rock and buck against him, her lush breasts jiggling.

A twig snapped nearby, but Lilly didn't seem to notice. He turned to see if someone had come upon them. Lady Anne stood there with Mister Crowley's hands cupped tightly over her mouth from behind. Her eyes were wide as the moon, but she didn't turn away.

Lilly was obliviously rocking over his cock, her breathy moans increasing in volume. Crowley's eyebrow lifted, and Henry smiled, inviting him to witness the coupling. Without releasing Lady Anne's mouth, Crowley used his free hand to reach beneath her skirts and worked between her legs.

Henry thrusted forward, slamming his length, drawing a scream from Lilly's lips. When he glanced back toward Crowley and Lady Anne, the woman was on the ground, skirts around her waist, and her legs draped over Crowley's shoulders. Her back arched so to allow her head to flip and watch them. The gent buried his hilt in Lady Anne's cunny, and pumped desperately, his eyes never leaving Lilly's ass.

Henry worked Lilly's slippery little pearl harder in time with his thrusts.

Lilly reveled in the movement's ecstasy. Henry's length inciting her into a higher state of lust. Just when she thought the feeling could not build anymore, the uneven moans and cries of the other couple nearby sent her flying over the edge. With another powerful thrust, Henry groaned and retreated from her. Lilly fell to her stomach in heavy gasps, feeling hot spurts of Henry's seed splash on her backside.

She lay there, face down, breathing hard, until her mind came back to focus. Anne and Crowley. She heard the cries of passion and the scream of release. The sounds were closer than before, Lilly was certain. She froze, not daring to move least they hear her. Then, she heard whispers and giggles and the distinct sound of running feet.

Lilly sat bolt up. "Do you think they heard?" She nervously scanned the darkness.

"I certainly hope so."

And it shocked Lilly to realize that so did she. Something awakened within her, a feverish need to explore all life offered. All her passions. She smiled seductively. "As do I, my lord. As do I."

Lilly slid across the reticule; two things clutched in her hands. The invitation from Lady Pettiford and The Gents I Plan to Bed—a list of her former suitors. If Abingdon could give her so much pleasure, she could only imagine what could be in store for her when she sought out the others. Her recent annoyance at her need to spend a few weeks at Devonshire House in London turned to pure excitement. London, and more specifically Whitterfield's sounded like the perfect place to start.

"Perhaps I'll see you in London, Mr. Crowley." Anne's voice sang musically as she entered the carriage.

Heat flushed across Lilly's cheeks, thinking the couple likely heard her bedsport with the earl—if coupling out of doors, out of bed, could be called such.

"You look absolutely radiant this morning, Lilly." Anne flashed her a most beautiful and approving smile, and Lilly knew immediately that her friend had heard. But Anne said nothing on the matter, so neither did she.

"I assure you," Anne said, "we will have a brilliant time in London. What have you decided about Lady Pettiford's invitation?"

Lilly opened the invitation and read carefully over the words. "I think," she hesitated, but then made her confession, "it's time for me to discover what fun widowhood could be. After all, how will I know what I like, if I do not sample offerings?"

Anne beamed. "I've so much to show you."

"How much could you have seen? You've been a widow for merely six months."

Her friend leaned forward. "When you join the ladies' club, you shall see for yourself."

Lilly fiddled with the other folded parchment in her hand. "I... um... made a list."

"Oh dear. Do you recall the last time you made a list? The one of all the forbidden books you'd read?"

She remembered. Anne and she had entrenched themselves in many troubles procuring the texts. Lilly hadn't made lists in years, but it was her thing when she was a young girl. Lists. Tangible goals. Once she set her mind to a task, she'd stop at nothing to achieve it. That was long ago, but oh, how she missed her younger, carefree, bolder self.

Anne's hand shot out. "Let's have it."

Lilly handed the page to Anne. She opened it, her eyes growing wider as they scanned the page. Then she leaned against the back of the seat. "My dearest friend, this is a wickedly delicious place to begin."

The End, or shall I say, 'twas only the beginning.

Also in the Duchess Diaries Series

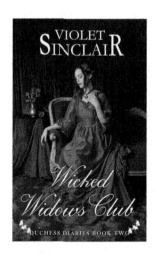

VIOLET SINCLAIR

The dowager Duchess of Devonshire's return to London high society is a fabulous one indeed when she accepts an invitation from Lady Pettiford to join an exclusive club of free women. The old countess runs the secretive Lady's Side, hidden behind the walls of the famed Whitterfield's gaming hell. Here the widowed women of the ton are free to pursue every pleasure—with their money, their desires, and most importantly—their bodies.

London's season of royal splendor and hidden debauchery is beginning. The ladies and gentlemen of the ton are flooding into town eager to mingle and posture, for gossip and scandal. Debutantes prepare to preen and attract proper husbands. And the Duchess has an agenda of her own. Awakened to her sensuality and sexual cravings, Lilly boldly explores new sensations and lustful fantasies in the pursuit of fulfilling her wicked list.

Available in paperback, ebook, and Audible at Amazon.com

About Violet Sinclair

Violet Sinclair is obsessed with all things historical ballrooms, fancy gowns, and Regency England. When she's not traveling the world with her boys, you can find her  writing sexy stories and dreaming of her next journey poolside beneath the Florida palm trees.

Printed in Great Britain
by Amazon

37030299R00047